Evincepub
Publishing

EVINCEPUB PUBLISHING

Parijat Extension, Bilaspur, Chhattisgarh 495001
First Published by Evincepub Publishing 2020

ISBN: 978-93-89988-57-4
Price: 149 ₹

LOVE IN THE TIME OF CORONA VIRUS

When nature turns in mood of revenge …

Part - 1

KAWALPREET KAUR

MESSAGE FROM AUTHOR

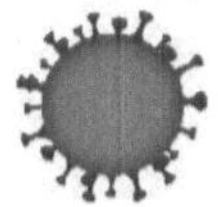

I am immensely grateful that this book is in your hands. I deeply expect that this book serves the full expression of the grief and makes an emotional connection with the people who lost their lives during the pandemic covid 19.

Many lost their love, family and even parents. The world has changed drastically for many of us as it was 3 months ago. A lot has changed.

I dedicate my book to those doctors, nurses and patients who have been standing tall in between the rest population and the deadly pandemic coronavirus and are courageously fighting with zeal to defeat it. It took me a lot of exploration and days and nights of hard work in creating it for you all.

I have given all I have in writing of this book. I greatly thank all the very good people around the planet who stood for each other in this hard time. With full heart and soul I dedicate this book to the heroes that are present inside every one of us but a few come out to protect the world.

Last but not the least as my mother says

"Earth stands alive, only because of good people"

With love,
Kawalpreet

ABOUT THE AUTHOR

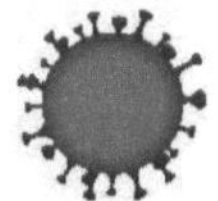

Kawalpreet Kaur is a highly inspiring 26-year-old Vice Principal of St Xavier's Mirzapur.

She has 6 wonderful years of experience in teaching. She is an M.Sc (botany) gold medallist and a governor awardee.

Apart from this, she as a person enjoys road trips, singing, playing and exploring new places.

Lawyer cum vice principal by profession but an author by soul.

"To each and every one who has lost their life in the pandemic coronavirus and to nurses, doctors and staff who stood for all of us"

ACKNOWLEDGEMENT

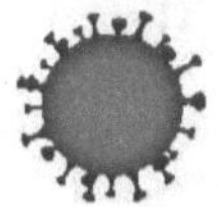

It's always great to write an acknowledgement. A lot has changed in 10 years but I am glad that true love still exists leaving behind the tinder relationship these days.

I will begin by thanking the real-life Skystar and their friends Gracy and *Shrey* who helped Skystar during their journey.

Special thanks to my mom (*Davinder Kaur*) for encouraging and motivating me. I would also like to thank my sister (*Preet*) for being with me throughout the journey.

I would also like to thank a few important people who have helped me while writing the book – *Gracy, Nayanika, Ajay, and Vishal.* This won't be possible without their feedback.

I would also like to thank my publishers for extraordinary kindness and having faith in me as being a first-time author, I was very nervous. Thank you for being so supportive!

Thanks to all the readers for having faith in my book. I am representing my heart and soul in the book. Hope you all like it. It took immense hard work for me to write this book.

This may be just a book for you but for me it is a result of my sleepless nights and hours of sitting on chair researching and putting in emotions.

Thank you! 

CONTENTS

1. Pehli mulakat   1

2. Ye kaise hua   5

3. Humari adhuri kahani   10

4. Kuch toot sa gaya hai   16

5. Pyaar, mohabbat sab dhoka hai   20

6. Fir udi mai   28

7. Ek nayi duniya banayenge hum   34

8. Tum firse choot na jana   42

9. Mere hisse ki khusi tum ho   51

10. Coronavirus outbreak   57

11. Chronology of events occurred during coronavirus   65

12. Peace   74

Know more about coronavirus   77

KARMA SAID

"Sometimes you have to suffer in life, not because you were bad, but because you didn't realise where and when to stop"

PART 1

PEHLI MULAKAT

There was a decathlon cycle race at India Gate, New Delhi. Being immensely excited for the race I woke up before time, got myself ready and reached the store where I completed the registration work and got a blue shiny bicycle. As soon the whistle blew, I started paddling the cycle and a flashback of my life came in front of my eyes. I went back to 2012 summers – my class IXth journey, the red bicycle I had, the school and friends.

Hey but before going ahead, I forgot to tell you about myself. My name is Siya and I belong from a high-class Sikh family where pride and honour come first. Girls of our family were not permitted to do what they wished but what is right according to the society because my father always used to narrate the same slogan in my ears *"log kya kahenge…!"* I still remember how the twist of my life came in 2012.

It was April, a new beginning to a new session. Having a few close childhood friends like Gracy and Shrey, life was fun. We were having a great time at school until one day things began to change. I never thought 2012 would be a year to remember forever.

It was boring a maths class; Miss Jennifer was solving ratio and proportion questions, and at the back bench, me and my friend Gracy were laughing and giggling. We heard a loud voice to our ears "go out of the class the last bench girls." As we walked out of the class a strong smell began to attract me. I saw a tall, handsome yet shy boy standing out of section B of Class IX. We both looked at each other's eyes like we knew each other from years. His black eyes were shining like a star. The smell of his body was making me crazy. I could not understand what was it, was I a vampire? Like the Twilight movie. I laughed at my own thought and the bell rang.

We went back to class.

Few days later, my friend Shrey advised me to join chemistry classes as I was weak in studies and boards were heading close. As the tuition was very far from my house, it took days to convince my mom to let me go.

I still remember that shimmering evening around 6pm when I reached the classroom and that strong smell began to stick to my nose again. As I entered I saw Shrey and that section B boy was sitting and studying. I said "Hi", he ignored. I found him very rude to me but later got to know that he was very shy and not rude.

After a few days of regular meetings made him open in front of us, and finally the day came when he said "Hi, I am Shravan Kumar Yadav" I smiled. After talking and analysing him, I found him calm and very introvert – the exact opposite of my personality.

We both were like either side of a coin – one was calm as a breeze and the other was stormy as cyclone.

"Be thankful for what you have in life because you never know when it will be taken back from you"

PART 2

YE KAISE HUA

Love stories in 2012 were very different from today's love stories – the tinder dates to practical and ambitious couples. The love stories of that time were not at all practical rather very emotional.

Hence the days went by and we became much closer. We started talking for hours. We became addicted to each other and loved to spend together round the clock. Our morning used to start early at 7 am after which I used to ride my bicycle up to the railway colony where he used to wait for me and we after meeting used to ride and talk till we reached the school. As we were from different sections – A and B, we could not talk to each other, but as the first benches of both the classes were visible to each other, so we used to fight with others for taking that particular seat.

As a result, the friends who used to sit in the first bench were very much annoyed with us, which we were least bothered. But it was amazing not only for others but also for me that the one who never preferred to sit in the first bench till the last date is now fighting for that seat.
From 3 pm to 7 pm we had tuitions and then we used to ride our bicycle back home. After coming back also, we used to think about each other. We used to write letters thinking of the other one.

Those days' mobile phones were not so popular. On Sundays when we used to have off from school and tuition, he would call on my father's phone at 10 am from a PCO just to hear my voice. It seemed like we had a large stock to discuss and so cannot waste a single minute and wanted to be together every time.
Days went by until one day when we were riding back home after tuition, my friend Shreya told me that Shravan wanted to say something. I looked back and said, "What?"

He smiled and said, "ILU" and ride his bicycle as fast he could.

I even could not understand what he wanted to say until the next day when I got to know "ILU" meant I love you. That time "I love you" was a big word and people used to treat it as some ghostly thing.

We started seeing each other and he used to follow me everywhere, even to my Scooty classes. He started teaching me how to ride Scooty. I was riding the Scooty and he was sitting on the back seat, and suddenly a small lip touched my cheek; that was my first kiss …

I warned him for that and left the class; after that incidence, I started ignoring him, I knew my family and the things how horrible it will become. I was scared of the outcome. I joined another history coaching nearby my house, until one day. The doorbell rang, ma'am told me to open the door. To my surprise it was none other than Shravan.

He smiled and said, "Ma'am may I come in." ma'am said, "You are late, come in and open your books."
I was shocked but inside I was feeling peace, my heart was beating fast and my eyes were watching only him. My mind said this bloody stalker is stalking

me but my heart supported and said, "He came just because of me."

As the class ended, we moved out of the room to the stairs and suddenly he held my hand and went on his knees and said "Siya, I ... I ... I ... wanted to say ..." as he was sweating.

I ... wanted to say, "I love you" ... he took the ring which he bought for me and placed on my ring finger. He promised me to love me forever and I was so touched with the feelings that we both hugged each other. As his hands began to tighten, our heart pumped faster and breathes were high ... We both had no words to utter, just held the hands together.
I came back home and wondered "Ye kaise hua ...!"

"He who fears will always suffer because they are already suffering from their fears"

PART 3

BREAKUP PART 1 – HUMARI ADHURI KAHANI

The next day I was blushing as I waited for him near the railway colony. After meeting in the usual place, we without saying anything started cycling towards school. Like me, he too was blushing. This was the teenage love. In the evening we went to the history class and like a normal routine used to spend time together on the stairs, hugging and holding hands of each other.

He used to sit at back of my seat and touched my feet from his feet. These silly things of him made me blush and made us realise what love felt like. I remember, once I fell ill and could not attend the school. After 2 days of high fever, I requested my parents to let me go to the history class. I told my mom that I didn't want to miss my classes and went to class. That day as I entered the stairs of the class, a hand pulled me closer and I heard him breathing very close to me.

He hugged me tight and began to cry. He confessed that he missed me a lot and could not even describe how he spent these days without me. That day we didn't attend the class but sat on the stairs talking for hours and went back home with the promise to meet next day. He used to mark benches with Sky (Shravan Kumar Yadav). I asked him, "If you are Sky, then who I am?" He said, "You are my 'star.'"

And hence we started calling each other Skystar. Mobile phones were very rare to those days for students. He bought an old second-hand mobile so that we could talk at night. One night my mother heard me talking to somebody. After that, she started a search operation of the device by which I was talking. But all thanks to God that she could not find my mobile. The same happened with Sky too but he was not so lucky like me.

He was caught with the mobile and his mother broke the mobile into pieces and warned him too. The happy couple had started facing the tough world, the world which was against any boy and girl who were friends or any type of relation. I remember that horrible day when I was going to Lucknow for 6 days, it was the first time that I was leaving him for so long. Being a single soul we could not live apart from each other for a long time so we made a plan of meeting at the stairs of history classes. But that became a nightmare for both of us. We were hugging each other so peacefully that we did't heard our teacher coming, As she shouted "what are you doing here?". We rushed out of the stairs to our home. But we were unaware that our life was about to change.

I went back home. Next day in the early morning, I saw the teacher talking to my father and was informing him about me and my Sky. My father called me and asked me about him, which I straight away denied. I knew that outburst if I accepted. But little I knew that my denial will result the same. A hard palm was moving towards my cheek He slapped me very hard and continued to ask the same, which I kept on denying. He repeatedly asked me the name of the boy and I kept on denying, and the next day my father sent me to Lucknow – 6 long days without him were so terrible.

Once I came back home I wanted to meet him, talk to him, confront him once, how was he? And then my father told me to come with him. We were walking towards his house. Gradually I was getting very scared and finally when we arrived at his home, my heart jumped out.

My father took us inside where his parents were already sitting. There my father told his father, "Your boy stalks our daughter, and if he didn't stop, I have to inform the police and make him arrested." Sky mother was very surprised and angry. She asked Sky what the matter was. He didn't speak a single word, resulting the same which I received 6 days earlier. She slapped him hard and told him to swear not to talk to me again.

Everything ended! I went to school the next day where I saw him. I tried to contact and talk to him but he started avoiding me. Missing him, I used to see the ring every time that he presented me. I wore it every time and recalled him. I missed him badly and cried hard. Once I pleaded hard to my friend Gracy to arrange a meeting with him. She finally called him to the stairs of the school.

I still remember, I was standing in front of the physics lab when I heard him coming. I began to cry

after seeing him. I told him not to leave me. He said nothing and so I became angry and returned his ring to him and said, "If you loved me ever you will return this ring to me."
What I expected didn't happen.

We broke up! ☹

I was not able to focus on my studies and I failed and left the school.

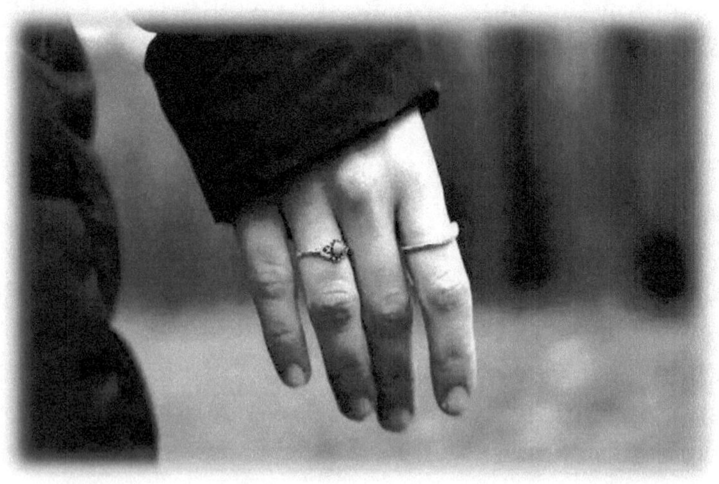

"Experiments are necessary for the experience that creates growth and new opportunities"

PART 4

KUCH TOOT SA GAYA HAI

Things became worse for me as people started judging me and my character just because I was on the stairs of history classes with a boy. Yes, we still live in that world where a boy and a girl walking or talking together are seen with big eyes and girls judged as characterless.

My father was facing humiliation just because of me. I was not allowed to go out alone. I was jailed in my own home. I was then sent to a private school where it was not compulsory for me to attend the classes. I was treated as I had made a major sin. I lost Sky, the love of my life. I was devastated. I felt cheated that he could not even stand for me.

All love was just an attraction. I used to cry all day. Seeing my condition my mother send me to a computer class just to make me get out of home. But before letting me out of the house, my mother strictly told me to stay away from such nuisances, which I promised that I will.
It was day 1, I was wearing a blue suit. Respecting my mother's words or out of fear of outcome, which had already shattered my life, I entered the class keeping my face down. As I entered the class, I saw a tall boy standing. I thought he was the teacher, I said, "Sir, I came here for my classes." He gave me a chair to seat and started to interrogate "What is your name, girl?"

I replied softly keeping my head down "Siya."

A loud voice I heard, "Hello Siya, I am Manoj the class teacher and this boy is Ajay."

I kept quiet and the class started. Ajay was a funny boy. He belonged from a village area and was therefore he was very pure from heart. He started making me happy by his jokes. We used to spend time in classes together. He was very good in maths so he used to help me in solving problems. He started liking me, which I could feel when he was near me.

He used to do all stuffs just to make me happy but I didn't feel the same which he used to. It was 2013 New Year eve and the computer class organised a small party. That day I wore saree for the first time. We all were celebrating and then Ajay called me in the classroom. There were other students too. He just bent on his knees down and proposed me. And everybody there started clapping. I was very shocked and it was hard for me to breath. I just ran from there and cried a lot. All my past started flashing in my eyes. I missed Sky that day. The flashback of Sky–Star story again filled my life with tears and I left the classes.

*"Challenges are what make life interesting,
but overcoming the challenges is what
makes life beautiful"*

PART 5

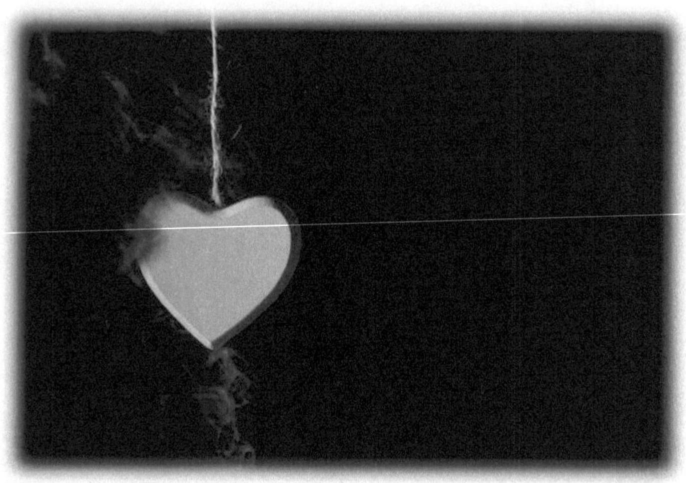

PYAAR MOHABBAT SAB DHOKA HAI

2013 started with a bad thing and became even worse for me. I found a friend in form of Ajay but lost him soon. The memories of Sky were always nurturing me. But my broken heart never tried to contact him.

I took admission in B.Sc department and my college journey started. It was day 1 of my college. As I entered the campus I saw so much crowd everywhere.

I asked my friend Shreya about it. She said, the college election was going to be organised soon. All these dramas were because of that. Our class started but soon was interrupted by a young, slim, and a very rude boy.

He entered our class and told the teacher to stop the class. He said, "My name is Vikram Singh and you all have to elect me the students' leader from of college, understood!" Unlike other politicians, he was not at all sober, but everybody out of fear nodded their heads in "yes."
I found him very rude and arrogant. I searched his profile on Facebook. Yes Facebook, the new thing which we had – a new way to communicate. He too was having a profile in it. I sent him a message, "You are very rude, you won't win."

The next day as I went to college to attend class, I saw him standing in front of the main gate. He came close towards me and I started to shiver. He said, "Why would I not win?" I said, "Sorry, Sir!"

He in an ordering tone offered me, "Come and spend today's day with me." I said, "Ok."

The whole day I was following him in each and every corner of the college. I saw him meeting all elders with respect and solving the issues of juniors. After spending the day with him, I found him the opposite of what I thought about him. My thought changed completely about him.

We started spending time together and soon I started campaigning for him. The social justice that he did started attracting me towards him. He tried his best to resolve the issues which he was notified of. The more I spent time with him, the more I got attracted towards him. I was loving the fame, popularity and respect he received from others, and above all his attitude.

At the time of campaigning, he used to drink tea with me and we used to talk about life and how we can improve the college.

Things were going fine. The Election Day came and as though he won. I was so happy that day. I congratulated him on Facebook. He messaged me to come home. I went to his home with my family. The celebration was on. Everybody was celebrating. He gave me a rose and said, "Thank you! And ... I love you.!"

I was just smiling, I had no words to describe. I just said, "I need time" and he hugged me tightly.

Things were moving so fast. Yeah, I knew him but I didn't know what he was thinking at that point of time. Maybe he was very happy and wanted to settle now.

The flashback memories of Sky again started to cover up my mind and I left his house with tears in my eyes.

We started spending time in the library and college canteen. I soon started enjoying his company. People and students used to treat him as a celebrity. I was happy that the world was mad for him but he was mad for me. This feeling was great! He used to bring roses, chocolates for me and often took me on rides. We started knowing each other better. He walked in the college with his red Apache bike like he owned the collage and I just sat and watched how people were getting mad seeing him. Girls wanted to be around him.

He was the hot topic of the year. His choices, the behaviour and above all his fight for justice made everyone his fan. As time passed one day he looked into my eyes and said, "You will marry me!" I said, "I haven't thought about it yet." He just stood up gave me a weird look and said, "I am not asking you, rather telling you!" I was shocked by his behaviour. None that I knew things were about to get worse.

I never said, I love him but we were still in some strange relationship where he was a king and I was the queen – but queen with no authorities. Slowly after spending more time with him, I understood his inner personality. He used to bully me, didn't allow me to go classes, and checked my phone constantly.

He used to make weird comments on my dresses and sometimes on my body too. I began to feel trapped in the relationship until one day. I still remember that day I was about to accept my feelings for him and tell him to change himself, otherwise I will leave him. I went to the college to confess what I felt for him as I was waiting for him in the canteen. I saw a strange message on my phone "Hi, do u know Vikram?"
I replied, "Yes."

She said, "Leave him, he is my boyfriend for the last 4 years."

I was very much shocked; I saved her number and asked her to meet me tomorrow. All my love feelings vanished. The pain I had when Sky left me hugged me again. I was feeling the same pain again. I was shattered.

The next day I met the girl. Her name was Priya, she showed me some of her pictures and videos with Vikram. She said, "He used me and also many more other girls. He just wants to win the election by making commitment to the girls. But he proposed me after elections, after listening to her my inner mind lost peace." Priya cried hard as I tried to console her. I messaged Vikram not to message me again and blocked him.

The next day I found him calling from another number and narrating his story. I replied him with disgust, "I d...don't want an explanation," but he insisted to meet once.

As for the last time, I agreed to meet him at the library.

I reached college at 8am in the morning waiting for him. He walked in with a gun in his hand. He said angrily, "You can't leave me, I will kill myself and all blame will be on you."

I started shivering and crying. I said, "You are already in relationships with many girls. Kindly leave me alone!"

He said, "Nobody can leave me, I can only leave girls."

That day I got to know the other side of him. I was so scared, I pleaded to let me go. He put the gun on my head and said, "I told you, nobody can leave me."

As the librarian entered the room, he asked, "What is happening?", and I ran out of the room and ran out of the college to my home. I switched off my mobile and cried very hard. Tears rolled down my eyes. I was all alone. Nobody was there with whom I could share my emotions. In the evening, my mother entered the room and asked what the matter was, I could not stop my tears and told everything to her. Noticing the seriousness of the situation, she booked my tickets to Mumbai where my masi used to live.

The next day I found myself leaving the city, leaving my school, my college, my friends, my family and Sky memories.

"Heart was made to be broken"

PART 6

FIR UDI MAI ...

I came to Mumbai things were so different here. After 2months, I had my last semester exams I had to study but my mind was taking me back to the memories and things that happened few days before.

The Sky was darker that morning, as if in mourning. Sitting on the floor I was finding my clothes to wear for that day, as a calm voice was heard "Hi sweetie! Do you need anything?"

I said, "No." and took out my books to study. Till then I was an average student but things had to change now. I opened the book and started going through my syllabus. Time went by and one day I requested my masi that I wanted to go to the beach. After seeking permission from her, I booked an Ola.

Soon I was on beach. The waves were rolling heavily. I kept on moving and crossed the safety mark, the divers stopped me from going close to seashore.

I looked around to see if I was only one there.

Water was flying with the wind. It was raining like cats and dogs. I should not have expected to see anyone at this weather at the beach. The condition of the weather was not bothering me at all.

As the waves started touching my feet, the memories of my life began to haunt me again. Pouring water and sound of thunderstorms and clouds too couldn't budge my memories.

As the rain droplets were kissing my cheeks, I saw a boy beside me covering up both of us under the umbrella.

He said as softly as he could, "It's raining heavy ma'am, not a good idea to stand here."
I looked at him and said nothing.

He continued, "I have a cafe shop near the beach, would you love to come for a cup of coffee?" I smiled and followed him to the cafe.

He brought a hot cappuccino with a teddy bear designed on it. I smiled as he bought his cup of tea and sat opposite to my bench. "You look new."

I smiled, he said, "Either you don't talk much or you avoid talking to strangers."

He continued, "Hi! I am Shubh."

"Hi, I am Siya." and I opened my mouth.

He started telling me about the beauty of Mumbai, that he was brought up here and the places to explore here. I was just listening to his talks as I was searching for money in my purse.

He said, "Paise nahi chahie."

I asked, "Why?"

He said, "I don't charge to beautiful girls."

The flirting lines stuck to my heart and made me laugh. He too smiled. Then we both passed smiles to each other. I said "Bye!" as I left the cafe shop.

I didn't even look at him and moved out. I didn't want to begin a new chapter now nor wanted to face the things relationship gave me.

As the rain hasn't stopped yet, I started searching for auto. My phone too has become dead. Leaving the hope to book an Ola, I started searching for auto until I heard that stranger again.

"Hey I am going towards Andheri, do you want me to drop you somewhere?"

'No, thanks." I replied.

He continued, "Trust me, it's no bother."

I smiled as I put my bag inside the auto first and entered. I sat at a distance from Shubh.

As he continued, "There are two things that are difficult to find in Mumbai – flats for singles and autos and cabs in monsoon."

I agreed, but you missed one thing, I said with a smile on face.

"You don't even get peace in Mumbai." He looked at me and said "Peace doesn't come from outside, but it lies within us. Peace doesn't come when you get what you wanted but comes when you get what was good for you, what was made for you."

I smiled as if I understood the meaning of peace but little did I know that my peace was lost long ... long ago.
As I reached home ... I said "Thank you" taking a deep breath.
"Bye," he said.

"No matter how much suffering you went through you never want to let go memories"

PART 7

EK NAYI DUNIYA BANAYENGE HUM

I came home, and after changing my clothes I started searching jobs for graduates so that I could take off the extra burden I was carrying. I wanted to restart my life.

After searching for hours, I landed with a few decent ones. I finally submitted my resume to some call centre jobs and went for sleep. When I woke up I saw a notification on my phone. I avoided it and walked towards my masi's room, where we had a cup of tea and talked about how hard life was.
After taking the life's lessons I was getting ready for the gym. I checked the notifications which I saw after I woke up.

It was a message for an interview the next day from the call centre I applied for. I was happy to get a good response and told my masi about it. We both finalized my dress for the next day and started discussing regarding the interview and the questions that may be asked.

My masi asked me to introduce myself.

I did and many more questions I rehearsed for the interview.

I woke up early that day and got ready to go. I took a paratha in one hand and started moving out of the building. My cab was already waiting for me. As I stepped in I said, "Bhaiya address pata h na." For which he said, "Google pe show kr rha hai madam." The place was very far and new to me, so I verified from the driver.

And my journey started. I went to the office but my heart was pounding. I didn't know why but my heart was beating faster. I thought it may be because it was my first interview so I was feeling tensed. But the wind blew with warmth in it. My breath began to deep, I asked for a glass of water from the person standing there. As he gave me the glass of water with his turning towards me, my world turned around.

That smell again started attracting me towards it. I saw him standing. He was no other than "Sky," the glass of water slipped from my hands as his hand touch mine. I could not utter a word. My eyes were filled with tears. The memories captured my soul. The memories took me back to the school days – from the day I first saw him, the tuitions, the stairs and the panic we faced. I said, "Sky" as tears rolled down my cheeks.

He too was shocked. He stood still in front of me, without uttering a single word. I could clearly see the pain in his eyes. After minutes of watching each other, as the sweeper requested "Kindly move a little so that I could sweep the broken glass!", we both came back to reality.

He said, "You came here for an interview?"

I nodded my head in affirmative. He said, "Kindly wait here, and you will be called soon."

As he left the room, I went to the washroom, looked at myself and cried a lot because I could feel the same pain grooming within me which I felt years back. I washed my face as I had to appear for the interview and I could not let my past ruin my future. I did my makeup again and got prepared myself for the interview. I tried my best to calm my inner me so that the past does not that's day interview.

I came out of the washroom when the girl in the reception called out my name,

"Miss Siya you can go inside."

I said "Thank you" and walked towards the room.

As I entered the room I said, "May I come in sir?"
I saw Sky sitting there. He said, "Come in Siya." as he told me to come in, listening my name from his mouth was breaking me because Sky never used to call me by my name, he used to call me, Star … Everything inside was breaking – my mind and heart were going out of control, my hands were shivering.

As he said "Siya, can you introduce yourself?"

My memories took me back to 2012 summers where he was writing his name on the bench and engraving it as Sky. As I asked "If you are Sky then who am I?"

He smiled and said, "You are my Star" and we started laughing.

Again Sky interrupted, "Introduce yourself?"

My tongue started to salivate more, I took a deep breath and looked down the floor and introduced myself.

He then asked me, "What comes first to you – money or your reputation?"

The dark memories again captured me and took me into Sky's house where his mother, just for the sake of reputation, was telling him to leave me. I was sitting in front of him and sobbed as he chose his reputation above my love.

Sky again repeated, "I asked you something, Miss ...?" I replied "reputation" promptly, though with anger in my eyes while looking at him.

He told me to wait outside because he too could not control his emotions. He too I believe was in deep pain. He too may be felt the same, which I was feeling.

I was sitting outside remembering the moment we spent together. I was thinking how could life be so rude to me, Sky was my first love, my innocent love, how time passed so fast, why are we meeting again? What is still left to see as my heart was weeping from inside? My soul was again damaged.

I heard the receptionist calling out my name "Siya, you are hired, here is your offer letter" and she smiled. I took the letter and walked out of the office. I came out of the office and sat just in front of a tea store wondering what happened? And why it happened? As I saw from the mirror glasses Sky was watching me from his office.

We both looked at each other, even when the distance between the two was high but somewhere I saw the Sky–Star, the innocent couple holding hands and hugging each other and crying. I wiped my tears off and my imagination too.

I walked out of the area and again reached the beach cafe, where I met Shubh again.

He smiled watching me and said "What happened sunshine?" as he said the line, it began to rain heavily. He looked at me as I was the Goddess of Rain and as soon I arrive in the beach it started raining.
He looked strangely towards me and said, "Are you sad today? Is it the sky that is weeping or the clouds that are crying? Or is it you who made them sad?"

I smiled and said, "Can I get a coffee?"

As he brought coffee for me, I said, "I got a job Shubh." He smiled in response and said, "Wow Siya that's a good news!" I took a deep breath and said, "My boss is my ex!"
He kept quiet for a moment and said, "That's ok, it's life. Such things happen, you should definitely do the job because it will take out all your worries and love for him. ...Do you still love him?"

As he said those lines, my heart began to beat faster. It took me back to the stairs of my history class where I was standing and he bending on his knees said, "Siya, I wanted to say I ... I ... I .... and I replied him "I love you!"

Those lines began to echo inside my mind "... I love you Sky, I love you ..."

As Shubh touched my hand, I came back from my imaginary world. I said "Thank you" and moved out of the café shop. I even forgot to say "Bye" to Shubh. I was again sitting on the beach realising that life is so hard. What I always wanted I never got, what I didn't want came in front of me.

The story of my life was quicker than my pulses. Sometimes life is so cruel to us, little did I know that it was going to be worse soon.

"Past beats inside me like a second heart"

PART 8

TUM FIRSE CHOOT NA JANA ...

I started working at Sky's company, days turned into weeks and weeks turned into a year. We didn't interact except the work that too I wished to avoid but was compelled as he was my boss.

It was very hard for both of us to face each other but we both wanted to see each other every day. He did little things that proved that. Whenever I used to get absent, I always got a call from my senior regarding my well-being – "Was I ok?", "Was everything fine?", "Whether I am ill?"

These general concerns were not from side my seniors but from the side of Sky, which I knew very well. We never talked with each other but we never stopped caring until things started to become worse. 2019 November …

We all gathered for a meeting with the boss. As he entered everyone said, "Good morning, Sir!" He wore a black shirt, with folded sleeves. I never told him but black suits him.

He started the meeting, "Good morning everyone, as you all know we have gathered here to discuss the progress report, as we know the calls which we receive are for the benefit of the customers, but recently there was an increment in the international calls, the customers are well satisfied with us, and as the gesture of thanks, company wants to give its employees a free trip to China for a week." Listening that everybody started clapping and had a smile on their faces.

"So we will be leaving on Saturday and returning back to work with more energy. Kindly fill the forms for tickets confirmation and start packing".

As he ended the meeting, everybody in the office was talking about his generosity and kindness, everybody was excited about it. I was in dilemma whether to go or not? It was late, I packed my bag and hurriedly moved out of office.

As I reached the lift and touched the open button, slowly the lift opened. I never knew whether the doors of the lift was opening or the doors of my heart were again opening for Sky. I saw him inside the lift. I put down my head and moved my legs backwards and pressed the close button as Sky stopped the lift and requested "Hey, you can come in."
I entered the lift quietly. He was looking at me continuously. His strong body smell again was stuck to my nose, and my mind took me back to memories of the first time I met him.

He softly said, "Are you fine?" These were his first 3 words of concern in a year of my working which were coming out of his mouth directly. He continued, "Are you going to China trip?" I kept quiet. He further added, "I am there for help anytime if you need." Back in my mind, the boy bent on his knees promising me to be with me appeared, the tears started rolling down my eyes.

I have never forgotten you Sky, you were always in my heart. The memories I created with you were always haunting me when you left me alone. Inside my mind I spoke loud, wanted to tell him what I buried within me.

As the lift opened I said nothing and moved out of the lift. Sky tried to hold my hand, but his hands couldn't touch me as the lift closed in no time.

Days went by and everybody was excited about the trip. Everyday China and the places to visit were the hot topic. Soon Saturday came, we all were ready with our bags.

It was evening, when I got a call from my senior to keep all medicines and necessary stuff. I knew who was telling me this. I smiled and kept my medicines. We all reached the airport on time; the happiness was visible at our faces. We slowly in line moved towards the Indigo international aeroplane. I had never travelled on a plane before so I was scared.

My heartbeat was getting higher thinking of the take-off. As I moved inside the plane, I searched for my window seat. The beautiful air hostess helped me to find my seat. After setting down, I plugged my earphones. I saw Sky coming towards me. I swiftly moved my stuff as he was going to sit beside me. My heart began to beat faster after seeing him this close, and I said, "Sir, will you be sitting here, can I sit somewhere else?"

He said "No, miss it's the seat number which we have got, and we have to seat according to it."

The plane came on the runway and my heart beats which were already running started participating in Olympics race. I was taking a deep breath to keep myself calm when I hold my hand tightly. I forgot everything and memories started to capture the situation, I saw the old school scene where I had my maths exam. I and Sky reached school early. As I was taking a deep breath, he held my hand tightly and said, "Siya come on, it's just an exam." I replied, "Sky it's not just exam its maths exam." He hugged me tightly and said "Hey, it's ok."

I heard that voice again while sitting on the plane. Sky said again, "Hey it's ok, calm down."

I came back from my imaginary world. It was a long journey – nearly about 12 long hours. Lights were turned off, snoring of some people could be heard clearly. As hours passed and there was nothing to do, I started looking out of the window. I turned by my side to see what Sky was doing. I saw him sleeping, the innocence on his face could not be described.

I kept looking his innocent face as his hand still holds mine. While looking at her, I could not remember when I slept, I woke up laying my head on his chest, rubbing my eyes. This was the peace Shubh was talking about, this was the peace which I missed every day, this was the peace which I felt after a long time. As I woke up, I still could see that Sky was still sleeping. Soon our destination arrived.

We moved out of the plane, it was a bright morning and everything was so beautiful there. We reached our hotel and had lunch. We all were getting ready to explore Wuhan – the business city of China. I believe China has not only boosted its economy but also the living standards of people. Drone police were everywhere to help and monitor.

We were to explore the seafood market today not because of the food but Sky wanted to show us the diversity of food Chinese eat. We also explored the toy train, the big malls, the grocery shops. It was 11 pm and we all were very tired. We reached the hotel where beautiful clean beds with soft and fluffy mattress were waiting for in our rooms. After the tiresome and long journey and eating such a delicious food, we all collapsed soon.

It was 1 am when I woke to drink water. My heartbeat and pulses were fast than usual, I was feeling like fever and dizziness when I heard someone talking outside. I opened the door and saw two of my colleagues talking. I inquired, "What happened? Why are you still awake?" One of them replied, "Sir is not feeling good, he just vomited." I thought nothing and rushed towards his room. I opened the door and asked, "Sir, are you ok?"

He smiled "Yes, I am good" as he laid down in his bed. "You go to sleep, a long day tomorrow."

I took a deep breath and asked "Are you fine?"

He nodded his head.

I closed the door and went outside towards my room. I was lying on my bed remembering the time we spend together. Soon I slept.

Early morning I enquired with a senior colleague after sir's well-being, they said he was fine now. I smiled and started getting ready for the day. I wore a floral dress and we all got ready to go on the trip. We were to explore the Chinese call centre today and there work ethics. We were to learn about their work culture and other positives, which could be implemented once we get back to work. I saw Sky standing there talking to the authorities. He looked fine.

After the tiring day, all were told to get back to the hotel for rest. As I walked out of the office, a hand pulled me inside the lift. It was Sky. I was in his arms. It became hard to breath. My memory lanes took me back to the history tuition stairs, where the same incident took place. He touched my cheeks and we both were looking into each other's eyes. I could feel it was not just my heart which was beating faster but Sky's beats too were running out of control. As he said, "Siya, will you join me for a cup of coffee?"

I collapsed in his arms, I lost my consciousness.

He kept shouting, "Siya ... Siya ... Siya ... What happened? Wake up Siya ..."

"Life will break you always"

PART 9

MERE HISSE KI KHUSI TUM HO

I reached the fairy wonderland where we both were still hugging each other. The next day when I woke up I found myself in the hospital. I saw Sky holding my hands.

I said, "Sir, what happened?"

He smiled but tears roll down his eyes. I asked him to take me to the hotel, but he denied. I asked him continuously what the matter was and why was he crying?

He said nothing, so I decided to move out by myself. As he was talking to the doctor outside my room, I swiftly changed my clothes and covering my face I moved out of the room. I saw Sky talking to the doctor. I ignored and started running towards the hotel. I booked a cab to my hotel.

When I reached hotel it was locked down, the people in white clothes were monitoring everything. I asked, "What happened?" They tried to explain but I couldn't understand their language.
As I walked out of the hotel I saw Sky running towards me. "Why you came here, come let's go!" as he held my hand. I told him, "What is happening? Will you explain?"

He forwarded the mobile to me to talk to my parents. I called mom and dad, they looked so worried. They asked with concern, "Where were you, Siya? It's almost 6 days you haven't called us. Are you fine? Is everything fine?"

I softly replied, "Yes I am fine, I lost my phone here, so I was not able to contact you. I will come back soon." As I hang up the phone Sky pulled my hand to the nearby vacant street and said, "Siya, all will be fine."

I looked at him "6 days, what happened to me? Was I unconscious for 6 days? Tell me, sir, what is happening to me?"

Sky said, "Hey trust me, everything will be fine, I am here for you."

I pushed him back and shouted, "Sky ... you are here for me, you ... who left me alone for the sake of family reputation, who even did not think once to explain me, you have destroyed me. I am in pain just because of you. I couldn't find peace just because of you" as I started crying.

He held both my hands tightly. He twirled my body making both our bodies one. The heat of his body touched mine; it made us forget about everything except the moment. My throat began to dry. He moved closer to me as he rested his hands up my hips. His manhood felt invigorated like never before, it felt great. It felt like two stormy rivers were meeting to settle their dispute.

Our bodies got hotter; there was no left space – even for air to pass between us as he tightened the grip on my back. I arched my mouth towards his. Slowly his hands ran towards my back and hips that gave me immense pleasure. The world around was fading out.

We both started breathing heavily and I surrendered myself to him. He held my face in his hands and pulled back my hairs and started kissing me badly. We were out of the world. We were kissing each other on the mid of the street, without even worrying about what would happen. He kissed me so intensely that I forgot all that he did to me. As it became hard for me to breathe I pushed him back.

He sat on his knees, "Star ... I love you" and took out the ring which I gave to him in class IX. He kept that ring safe. He continued, "I had died every day waiting for you, I tried to contact but my family pressure was very harsh on me. I was sent out of the town so that I could forget you and attend my graduations peacefully. In the midst of my graduation, I came back to our home city to find you, but after seeing you with Vikram in your college, I thought of not disturbing you. I thought, you might have found your happiness in him. I didn't want to disturb you, so I walked away silently. But when you came to Mumbai and sent your resume to our company, I enquired about you. I got to know what happened to you and the reason why you left city and came to Mumbai. It's all my fault I know. Please give me one last chance, please!"

He further added, "I too have lost peace the day I left you, you were always in my memories. Star please forgive me" as he began to cry loudly.

As I gave my hand in his hand, he put the ring back to my ring finger. We heard lots of noise, lots of vans, ambulances rushing towards us.

I don't know who were they but they held me tight and took me in the ambulance, the hands of Sky slipped from my hands. I kept shouting "Sky ... Sky."

"Everything you do comes backs to you"

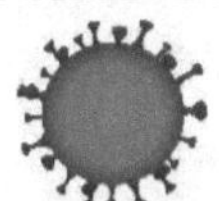

PART 10

CHRONOLOGY OF EVENTS OCCURRED DURING CORONAVIRUS

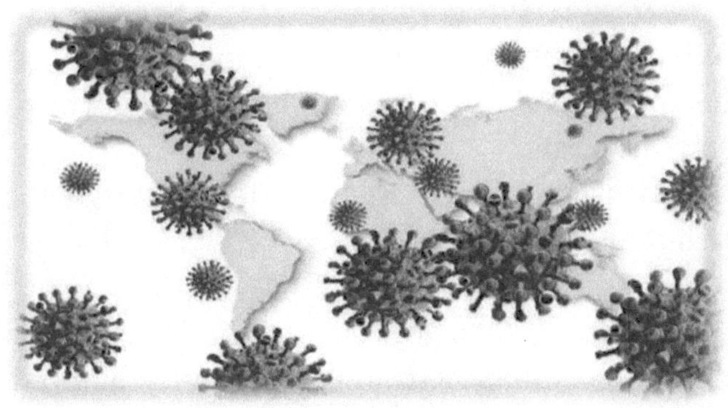

After taking me to the hospital, they injected me some medicines through which I became unconscious again. I woke up hours later listening to doctors' talk.

The blue suit doctors were testing me.

I asked them, "Hey doctor!" as hardly I could speak.

I asked again "What happened to me?"
Nurses uplifted me and doctors took me to the observation lab. They also told me that China is

suffering from some kind of virus, and I was just infected by it and as it is a communicable disease, I have been capped here.

I was not able to say anything and I asked "Doctor, where is Sky? The boy who was with me?"

The doctor replied, "As you were infected, the boy is also kept under observation that he might also be having the virus."
The doctor continued, "Keep patience, this will take time but everything will be fine."

In the initial days of suspicion of coronavirus outbreak in China, the Chinese authority had hidden the fact from the rest of the world. The authority has, remaining silent, allowed to spread the virus to grip the globe.

According to the sources and studies published in March, had Chinese authority informed the outbreak of the virus 3 weeks earlier, the affected numbers could have been reduced to 95% and a large part of the globe could have been safe from this pandemic.

The post of south China morning showed the delay China did to take a serious measure to protect from virus. The delay for about 3 weeks caused the infection to many.

As I researched in the phone, I found others too following the same timeline.

• December 10 Wei Guixian, one of the earliest known coronavirus patients starts feeling ill.

• December 16 Patient admitted to Wuhan Central Hospital with infection in both lungs but given resistance to antiflu drugs. Staff later learned that he worked at a wildlife market wherefrom he collected the outbreak.

• December 27 Wuhan health officials are told that a new coronavirus is causing the illness.

December 30

• Ai Fen, one of the top directors at Wuhan Central Hospital, posts information on WeChat about the new virus. She was reprimanded for doing so and told not to spread information about it.

• Wuhan Health Commission notifies hospitals of a pneumonia due to unclear cause and orders them to report for any related information.

December 31

• Wuhan Health Officials confirm 27 cases of illness and close a market they think is related to the virus spread.

• China tells the world health organization's China office about the cases of an unknown illness.

January 1

• Wuhan Public Security Bureau brings in for questioning the doctors who had posted information about the illness on WeChat.

• Official at the Hubei Provincial Health Commission Orders Lab, which had already determined that the novel virus was similar to SARS to stop testing samples and to destroy existing samples.

January 2

Chinese researcher maps the new coronavirus as complete genetic information. This information is not made public until January 09, 2020.

January 7
Xi Jinping gets involved in the response

January 9

China announced it has mapped the coronavirus genome.

January 11–17, 2020

• Important pre-schedule CCP meeting held in Wuhan. During that time, the Wuhan Health Commission insists that there are no new cases.

January 13

First coronavirus case reported in Thailand – the first known case outside China.

January 14

The World Health Organisation (WHO) announces Chinese authorities have seen "no clear evidence of human to human transmission of the novel coronavirus."

January 15

The patient who was the first one as confirmed to us to get affected by this disease leaves Wuhan and arrives in the US, carrying the coronavirus.

January 18

The Wuhan Health Commission announces four new cases.
Annual Wuhan Lunar New Year Banquet. Tens of thousands of people gathered for a potluck.

January 19

• Beijing sends epidemiologist to Wuhan

January 20

• The first case announced in South Korea

• Zhong Nanshan, one of the top Chinese doctors, who is helping to coordinate the coronavirus response, announces that the virus is communicable and can pass who are in contact or nearby to the infected person.

January 21

• United States centres for disease control and prevention confirms the first coronavirus case in the United States.

• CCP flagship newspaper people's daily mentions the coronavirus. Epidemic and xi's actions to fight it for the first time.

China's top political in-charge of law and order warns that "Anyone who deliberately delays and hides the reporting of virus cases out of his or her own self-interest will be nailed on the pillar of same for eternity."

January 23

Wuhan and three other cities are put on lockdown right around this time, approximately 5 million people leave the city without being screened for the illness.

January 24-30

China celebrates the Lunar New Year holiday. Hundreds of millions of people are in translate around the country as they visit relatives.

January 24

• China extends the lockdown to cover 36 million people and starts to rapidly build a new hospital in Wuhan. From this point, very strict measures continue to be implemented around the country for the rest of the epidemic.

• The bottom line
• China is now trying to create a narrative that it is an example of how to handle such crisis when in fact its early actions led to the virus spreading.

PART 11

CORONAVIRUS OUTBREAK

The disease was hidden out by the Chinese Government. It means that disease was spreading long before I reached China. Things began to become worse after 2 days, I saw Sky covering his body with a blue suit as we were in a glass chamber but we could each other here.

He said, "I am fine, how are you?"

I smiled "Are you okay?"

He cried "I am sorry, I left you, I destroyed everything. I brought you here and you suffered because of me. Please forgive me but I promise I will take you out from all these and make you reach safely to our home soon," he paused and after taking deep breath he said "Do you trust me?" The memories captured my mind again.

I remembered when I fell from bicycle and he was to apply Dettol and I was crying in pain, at that time too he said the same, "Do you trust me?" and I kissed his forehead and said "More than anyone can trust you." I came back from the memory lanes and smiled with tears in my eyes and replied, "More than anyone can trust you." and began to cry.

We both were crying from both sides of the glass chamber. I was coronavirus disease positive but it was quite a surprise for the doctors how Sky managed to be safe from the disease. For precautionary terms, he was advised to stay away from me. It was the month of February – Valentine's Day was approaching. The doctors decided a time when we could meet, but all the meeting could be held through a glass chamber, that too once a day.

We used to talk through video calls for hours and rest of time I was kept under the observation of doctor as the outbreak started to spread everywhere and things were getting worse.

The doctors were about to shift me in a severely critically ward. We spoke for the last time before I entered the room. I was not sure knowing whether I could survive this disease. The situation was getting more critical than we could imagine. We both were silent and then Sky just smiled and said "Will you marry me?" I was in tears but smiled too and said "No idiot, you leave me again." He kissed the glass of the room from his tight blue suit and from the covered mask he said "I will never leave you. I left you once and my soul lost its peace, I won't leave you now because after lots of pain I revived that peace again which I was searching for years. I will love you today, tomorrow and forever. You will be my star forever," he touched the glass while saying these words. Finally I replied, "I love you too."

I was taken to the room for further treatment. It took days for the doctors to operate. Time went by and it was March 2020. Almost 3 months we were still in Wuhan. I was switched to the normal observation ward. Everything was going fine when one day I heard someone crying.

As I watched out by my window, ambulance was taking away a body and that there was a lady and small child who were crying and weeping. Tears rolled down my cheeks too. Coronavirus has caused death of many loved ones. The outbreak destroyed many families.

There was no probability of our lives here. There were many peoples in worse condition than mine and many were seeing their loved ones dying every single minute in the hospital. People could not touch, could not hug, could not kiss them and bid goodbyes. Everything changed in a matter of time.

Few days past by and Sky kept on visiting me, but there was a line drawn between us – a glass chamber which was kept as a separation.

Doctors told Sky that my body was recovering but I had to maintain distance from others so that no one gets affected because of me. He was allowed to bring me back to home but a safe distancing had to be maintained till 14 days as there were chances that the virus can accrue again. If I survived this 14 days cycle, I could fly back home.

After 3 months of struggle and panic, I started living a normal life. I called my parents every day. When I was ill at that time China was the only city that was affected, but as soon as the WHO declared it as a pandemic, my family started worrying more about me as I consoled them every time that I was fine and will be back soon.

Then the day came when I wearing a blue suit with a mask on my face moved out the glass chamber where Sky was waiting in his blue suit. We hugged each other, though the suit was in between us. He held my hands and took me to the place where I was supposed to stay under observation for 14 days. We both were anxious about returning home as it has been a number of days when we were struggling with this disease – though Sky didn't show his feeling, I could interpret his behaviour and was in the same situation. He gave me a calendar so that I could mark these 14 days and return home.

We walked in the room; Sky showed me how he had designed the room. I looked at the glass door and said "Again!" He smiled "Only 14 days, sweetheart" and moved to the other side of the glass door.

And suddenly the voice echoed in the room. "Hey Star can you hear me?" Speakers were installed everywhere.

I said "I love you" a soft music began to play "Humko mili hai aaj ye khushian naseeb se" and I whispered coming close to glass door "Jee bhar ke dekh lijiye humko kareeb se." We both kissed each other from the glass door.

I removed my suit the house was protected as the rooms were designed by doctors of Wuhan for the patients who needed to keep social distancing so wearing the suit was not necessary in the house. T.V. channels showed the critical condition Wuhan was in. I still remembered the crowd, the beauty, the smile on face everything disappeared. The city was empty. 60,000 people left the city in 10 days. 80,000 people were still infected.

Many recovered many died!

As I was watching the news the glass door knocked. I asked, "Hey!"

Sky said "There is a window in your room I have kept soup, kindly have it."

I opened the window and took the bowl inside and closed the window. Sky spread the sanitizer on the windows around it as a precautionary measure. As I finished eating, he wore his suit back and took back the bowl and threw it in the dustbin and washed everything and sanitized everything. We were sitting on the other side glass door.

He used to wake up early and sanitized every corner of the house wearing that blue suit. He again started writing letters but this time digital one. We used to write as we were very far from each other but slowly we were coming closer.

Days went by and one day we both were talking on video call, Sky said "You know, what is the most beautiful thing in life?" I asked "What?"
He smiled and said "To have someone who loves you!"
I smiled seeing at his face and replied and that person you love is always safe and near you. As I remembered the time I spent in the hospital seeing family separating, people losing their loved once, children getting separated from their parents, the chaos, the noise, the screams, the pain. Thinking of those I started crying. Sky on the call said, "Everything will be fine, don't worry!"

And he hung up the phone. I laid down in my bed imaginary – the pain the family had gone through, the lost smiles .... Few minutes later, the glass door was knocked.

Sky said "I tried to make a chocolate smoothie for you." I went to the window to take it.

Sky began to sanitize everything, and meanwhile I had that yummy smoothie. 14 days passed and things getting worse everywhere; flights, trains, buses were cancelled. Cities were lockdown due to the fast spreading of the disease. 3,000 people died in Italy, the virus was spreading everywhere as I prayed to God joining my hands to give everyone the strength and peace so that they could soon recover the situation.

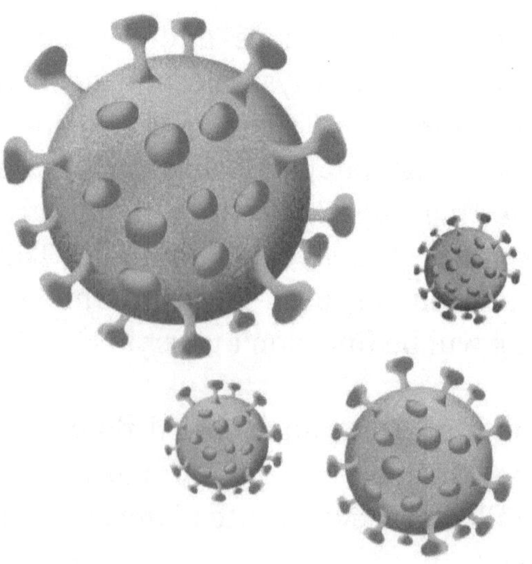

"We plan everything as we will live
forever but, destiny has its own plan."

PART 12

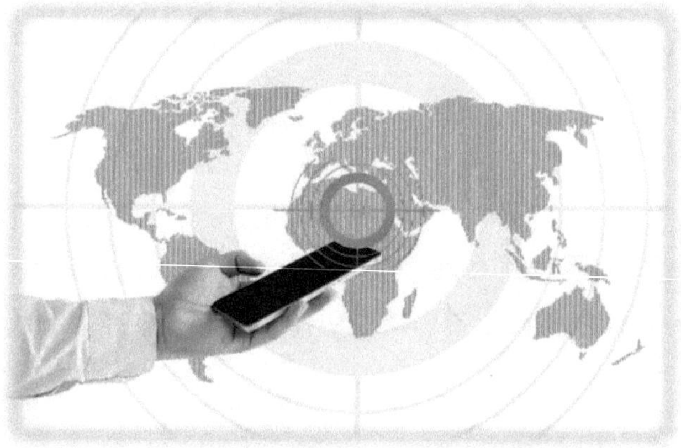

PEACE

The chronic scene ends and it is 2023 January. People from different parts of the world have gathered here to offer love and praise for the people who have lost their lives during coronavirus outbreak.

The decathlon race has been organised for the same reason as Siya was still paddling her bicycle. She all of a sudden comes out of her imagination of what all she faced by hearing a soft voice "Maa come on, you can do this, you can win this race maa!" It was none other than my 4-year-old son Navansh, holding his hand my husband cheering me up, Sky.

As Siya paddled faster, she not only won the race but her love from the pandemic coronavirus too, but alas! Many were not as lucky as Siya, the pandemic costs not only economic loss but emotional and mentally loss too.

Lives of several people changed forever and hence again the nature proved.

"We destroy nature, and nature has its own way to take its revenge!"

KNOW MORE ABOUT CORONAVIRUS

Coronavirus is an infectious disease caused by a newly discovered corona victim.

Most people infected from covid 19 will experience mild-to-moderate respiratory illness and recover without requiring special treatment.

Old people and those with underlying medical problems such as diabetes, cardiology and cancer are more likely to develop serious illness.

The best way to prevent and slowdown the transmission is to be well informed about covid 19, the disease. One can protect oneself and stop spreading to others from this infection by washing their hands or using alcohol-based sanitizer frequently and not touching their face.

Covid 19 virus can spread primarily through droplet of saliva or discharged from nose of an infected person. If he/she coughs or sneezes there is a possibility of spreading the disease, so every one of us needs to practice respiratory etiquettes.

Protect yourself, protect others!

"Nothing always stays the same, you don't stay happy forever, you don't stay sad forever."

〜